What about Me?

by Bracha Steinberg

Illustrations by Liat Benyaminy Ariel

Abba and Imma came home with our new baby boy today.

"Oh, look at his sweet face," said Bubby.

"What little hands. What little feet," said Zeide.

"What about me?" I thought.

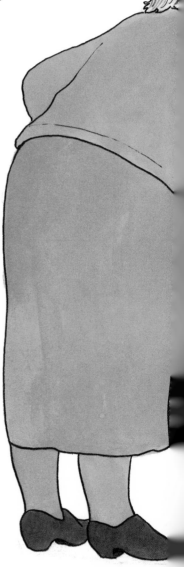

I wanted Imma to read me a book, but she said she had to go to bed.

"She's tired," said Bubby.

"She needs to sleep," said Zeide.

"What about me?" I thought.

Abba told me to go to another room to play.

I rode my hobby horse and wore a funny hat. It was fun.

But, when I yelled "Giddyap, Horsey! Giddyap" and ran around the room, everyone said, "Shhh! You'll wake the baby."

I sat down on the floor and thought, "What about me?"

What happened?

I used to be like a king here.

If I said "drink," Imma used to run to me with a cup of milk.

If I said "park," Abba used to run to put my hat on and take me out to the park.

Now the baby is king.

Everyone runs to him.

Everyone does things for him.

"What about me?"

Friday night, Abba made a *shalom zachor* for the baby. Many relatives and friends came to our house to help us celebrate.

We served *arbes* and cake and fruit and drinks.

Everyone said "*Mazal Tov*." Then they ate and sang *zemiros* and talked about the baby.

"What about me?" I thought.

Eight days after the baby was born, Abba and Imma and Bubby and Zeide and I got dressed in our *Shabbos* clothes.

Today is baby's *bris*, they told me.

We all went to *shul* with the baby.

My aunts and uncles and cousins were there and all of Imma's and Abba's friends were, too.

I saw a big, pretty, red soft chair.

"What's that?" I asked.

"That's a chair for Eliahu HaNavi. He's coming to the *bris* also," Imma said.

"What, is he coming too?" I thought. "Everybody is coming for the baby. But what about me?"

Zeide was the *sandak*. He held the baby while the *mohel* said a *brachah* and did the bris.

Abba also said a *brachah* and everyone else said they hope the baby grows up to learn Torah, raise a family, and do a lot of *mitzvos*.

After that, Uncle Shlomo held the baby and the *Rav* said a *brachah*. And the baby was given his name — David.

Everyone smiled and said, "*Mazal Tov*."

We all went to the *shul simchah* hall for the *seudah*. In one corner there was a pile of baby presents, wrapped in colored paper with ribbons. And the pile got bigger and bigger.

But I stood alone in a corner and felt very sad. I felt like crying. "What about me?" I thought.

When we got home, Abba and Imma opened all the presents.

I looked and looked to see if there were any for me.

There were little pants and little shirts, little hats and little blankets, little baby toys, like rattles and plastic ducks and frogs for David's bath.

"What about me?" I thought.

Then, I felt so sad that I began to cry and cry and cry. I was hurt because nobody paid any attention to me. I felt so bad that I lay down in the middle of the floor and just cried.

I kicked my legs and waved my hands. Everyone looked at me, but I couldn't stop crying.

"Whaaa! Whaaa!" I cried.

"WHAT ABOUT ME?"

My Imma came over to me. She seemed to understand.

"What about you?" she asked. "Would you like to see what about you?"

"Yes," I said, and I stopped crying.
Imma walked over to our bookcase and took down a very big book from the top shelf.

She sat down with me on the couch and opened the book on my lap.

I saw that it was full of pictures. Imma told me they were pictures of me when I was a baby.

There was a picture of me when I first came home with Abba and Imma.

There was a picture of Bubby holding me and Zeide looking at my little fingers and little toes.

There was a picture of the *mohel* I saw today at David's *bris*.

And there was a picture of me with lots of presents all around me.

I saw little pants and shirts and baby rattles and plastic frogs in the picture, and they were all mine.

I looked up at Imma and smiled.

"Do you remember the story I once told you about how Moshe Rabbeinu took care of his sheep?" she asked.

"Yes. You said that when he took them to a new field, he let the little ones eat the soft grass first. Then, the big ones went and ate the harder grass, and the biggest ones went last and ate the very hard grass that the other sheep couldn't chew."

"That's right," said Imma. "When Hashem saw that Moshe Rabbeinu knew how to take care of his sheep and give each one what it needed, He said 'Moshe is so good to his sheep. He helps each one get what it needs. I want him to be the leader of the Jewish people. He'll take good care of them, too.'

"Here, we try to be like Moshe Rabbeinu and give baby David what he needs.

"We run to feed him when he's hungry because he can't feed himself, as you can.

"We also change his diapers because he can't do that for himself, can he?

"And we carry him because he can't walk yet.

"But soon, he will get bigger. He will do more for himself. He will not need us to help him so much, just like you."

"I see," I said.

Now, when David cries, everyone still runs
to see what he needs.
"Maybe he's wet," says Bubby.
"Looks like he is," says Zeide.
And I still ask, "What about me?"

But now I say it so that everyone can hear me, because I want to help too.

And now everyone smiles at me and at each other as they wait for me to bring David a new diaper.

And today, when I gave Imma a diaper, do you know what David did?

He smiled a big, big, smile at me. So I told him that I'd let him be the king as long as he keeps giving me those big smiles.

Good Middos are the good traits the Torah tells us about — traits which help make us better Jews and better people. If we have good *middos,* we will always act, and say, and do things in the proper way.

But where can we find good *middos*? No one sells them or gives them away. We can only acquire them by looking and learning, by watching and listening. And by practicing.

In the **ArtScroll Middos Books**, you will find lots of interesting, exciting, fun-to-read stories with beautiful pictures. Each story will help you learn something new and important about **good middos.**

Enjoy!